Ruan
The Little Red Squirrel

This book belongs to:

....

Written by Rachel McGaw
Illustrated by Rowena Aitken

In the Highlands of Scotland,
nestled between great glens and long lochs,
there is a forest park that's home to some of the tallest trees you'll ever see.

And in those tall, tall trees in the forest park lives
a little red squirrel called Ruan.

Ruan loves living in his forest park.
He plays all day on the forest floor and in the tall trees,
chasing birds and butterflies.

Ruan and his friends are always full of mischief in the forest!

One day, Ruan and his friends come across some strange, brightly coloured bubbles in a clearing on the forest floor.
"What do you think they are?" asks Ruan.
"I know what these are,"
says Ruan's friend Ruby, peering out from behind a pine tree.

"These are called tents. They're what campers live in. I don't think we should go near them – they are for people, not for squirrels."
Ruan looks at the tents. Unlike Ruby, who is a shy squirrel, he's not scared of anything and certainly not afraid of being a bit naughty!

"I'm going for a closer look!"

says Ruan

Inside the tent, Ruan rustles through the campers' belongings.

He finds some chocolate at the bottom of a picnic basket that looks very tasty, but just as he is about to tuck in, he hears some much louder rustling coming from outside.

The campers are coming back!

Ruan jumps into the picnic basket to hide from the campers. He smiles, thinking that this little adventure into the tent is really rather exciting.

'Wait until I tell my friends that I nearly got caught'

But before he can scurry away, Ruan is shut inside the picnic basket

and packed up!

The campers collect all of their belongings and load them into their car, along with Ruan inside ...
As they drive away, Ruan sneaks a peek out of the back window and watches his forest park disappear into the distance.

"This might be more of an adventure than I thought..."
he says.

Little does Ruan know,
the campers are just starting their summer holiday.
The forest park was their very first stop

and now they are off on their travels

all over Scotland!

After a long drive in the car, the campers arrive at their next stop.
Ruan hides away again inside the picnic basket so that
the campers don't spot him.

Once the campers have set up their tents
and head off to explore,
Ruan peeps out from his hideout to see where he is now

Ruan sees some very, very big rocks – bigger than his tall trees at home. He looks around and sees lots and lots of water. He climbs out of the basket and spots a group of puffins flying high in the sky.

The puffins see Ruan on the ground – it's not every day that a little red squirrel turns up near the cliffs! Peggy the Puffin comes down to find out who he is.

"Hello," she says. "I'm Peggy. Who are you?
And what are you doing out by our cliffs?" she asks.
"I'm Ruan. I'm from the forest park. But now I'm lost and I think I'm quite far from home," says Ruan, looking a bit worried.

"Oh dear," says Peggy. "Would you like to stay here with us?"

She points up to her friends in the sky with her feathered wing.

"The cliffs are a great place to live. They are very steep, there are lots of nooks and crannies, and they're right next to the sea to catch lots of fish!"

Ruan looks around at the cliffs and the sea.

"It does look nice here," he says, "but there is something missing. **There are no trees! I don't think I can live here."**

Ruan waves goodbye to Peggy and scurries back to the car.

He curls up inside the picnic basket
and waits for the campers to return.

Maybe their next stop will be more like home.

The next day Ruan wakes to find he is in the beautiful countryside of the Scottish Borders. As far as he can see there are fields of green grass and yellow flowers.
Peering over the fence next to the campsite is Brodie the Beltie.

"Well hello there! What is a tufty wee fellow like you doing down in these parts?"

Brodie says.

"I'm from the forest park, but I'm lost. I think I am far from home."

Brodie tells Ruan, "You can stay here with me! Our fields are lush and green and very tasty. The farmer is always here to look after us."

Ruan scrambles up the fence and looks out across the farmland.

"It is lovely and green,"

"but so very flat."

"It does look nice here, but I don't think I can stay.

There are no trees!"

After another long trip in the car – and a pretty bumpy one at that – the campers' next stop looks even less like home.

Ruan climbs down from the car and lands on the sand.
It sticks in his tufty tail and he **doesn't like it!**

Ruan looks around and sees Sam the Seal basking on a rock.

"Excuse me," he says. "Where am I?
And what are all these bits stuck in my tail?"

"Well hello little one! Welcome to the Hebrides," says Sam.

"This fine stuff you're standing on is sand
and it's what the beach is made of.
What, may I ask, is a little red squirrel
doing here on the beach?"

"I'm lost,"
replies Ruan.

"And now I think I'm very
far from home!"

"Oh dear young chap," says Sam.

"You can stay here with me if you like. The beach is a brilliant place to live.
There are lots of waves to ride and fish to catch,
and lovely big boulders to sunbathe on."

Ruan looks at the beach and the rocks.
He looks out to the great blue sea.

"Thank you," he says,
"it does look nice, but I can't stay here. There are no trees!"
He leaves Sam to enjoy the sun and sulks back to his picnic basket hideaway.

After a long sleep and an even longer time spent picking sand out of his fur, Ruan peeps out of the car window and sees he is beside a long, wide river.

It's so much bigger than the burns and streams he is used to at home.

There is some grass on the ground, but it is very, very wet.

He looks along the flat river bank
and can already see there is something missing.

Oliver the Otter glides through the water and onto the river bank. He asks Ruan where he has come from.

"I've been all over Scotland," he replies.
"But my home is in the forest park. I'm not sure where I am now, but I think I'm very, very far from home."

Oliver puts a wet paw around Ruan.

"I'm sorry you're lost,"

"I would offer for you to stay here with me, but there really aren't enough trees here for squirrels. Our mighty river flows very fast, and I really don't think this is the place for you my friend."

Ruan nods his head. He wonders if he will ever find somewhere like the forest park.

Back in the picnic basket, Ruan rolls around on the back seat as he feels the car going up.

Up, and up, and up!

After a while the campers stop somewhere very high and very windy. Henry the Mountain Hare bounds over through the purple heather.

"**Hello!** I spotted your rusty red fur from all the way over there," he says.

"What is a little red squirrel doing **up here** in the mountains?" he asks.

"Oh," sighs Ruan. "I'm lost and I am very, very far from home. I don't think I'll ever get back to the forest park!"

"Well you could stay up here with me. There's lots of heather to keep you warm and great big mountains to climb,"

says Henry.

Ruan looks up at the mountains and then down at his little paws made for scrabbling up tress, not for climbing mountains like Henry's strong feet.

"They're very high indeed but I don't think I could stay.

There aren't any trees."

Feeling rather glum and very homesick, Ruan sets off back to the campsite. He tucks himself up inside the picnic basket and thinks of his home and his friends in the forest park.

He's missing home so much that he doesn't realise the top of his

tufty red tail

is sticking out of the basket lid.

When the campers come back from exploring the mountains, one of them spots Ruan's red tail.

"Goodness me!"

"A little red squirrel!
What on earth are you doing here wee one?"

Ruan peeks out from his hideout.

"Where could you have come from?"

she asks.

The campers think back over their holiday.

"He can't be from
these mountains,
there are **no trees** here,"
says one of the campers.

"He can't be from the
river bank
because there are no
trees there,"

says the other.

"He can't be from the beach because there are definitely **no trees** there! And he can't be from the farmland or from the cliffs,

because there are **no trees** there either."

The campers look at each other and then Ruan.

they ask.

"The forest park!"

"We must take
him home.
He needs to be
up in the trees,
not here in our
picnic basket!"

The campers pack up their car and let Ruan ride in the front seat. After a long drive down the mountain they reach the entrance to the forest park.

Ruan looks out of the window and all he can see are

lovely tall trees and bright green leaves and pines.

The campers stop the car where they had set up their tents a few days earlier and Ruan scurries out the door. He looks up at his beautiful forest.

"I'm home!"

The campers smile as they see how happy Ruan is scampering across the forest floor.

He brings them a nice big pine cone to say

thank you

for bringing him home.

Ruan darts up his favourite tree to find his friends.

"Ruan! Ruan! Where have you been?" they ask.

"I've been to the cliffs at the edge of the sea!"

"I've been to the fields of a farm!"

"I've sat on a sandy beach with a seal and a wet river bank!

And I've been to the top of a mountain!"

"I've been all over Scotland!" he says.
"And what was it like Ruan?" asks Ruby.

"Everywhere was beautiful,"

"and I met a lot of new friends who all loved where they lived."

"But for a little red squirrel," Ruan says...

"there's nowhere quite like home."

First published in 2016 by Forth Books
www.forthbooks.co.uk

ISBN 9781909266049
Printed in China